Have You Heard the Stories About FEAR STREET?

There are some stories always told in the dark—whispered from friend to friend. These stories give warnings about ghosts and other creatures of the night.

Zack Pepper has one of these stories, and his story happens on Fear Street.

Zack has a story to tell you about his substitute teacher, Miss Gaunt. Miss Guant lives in the Fear Street Cemetery—and she is looking for company.

Are you ready to hear Zack's story?

Also from R. L. Stine

The Beast
The Beast 2

R. L. Stine's Ghosts of Fear Street

  #1 Hide and Shriek

Available from MINSTREL Books

R.L. STINE'S
GHOSTS of FEAR STREET®

WHO'S BEEN SLEEPING
IN MY GRAVE?

A Parachute Press Book

A
MINSTREL®
BOOK

PUBLISHED BY POCKET BOOKS

New York   London   Toronto   Sydney   Tokyo   Singapore

A MINSTREL PAPERBACK *Original*

 A Minstrel Paperback published by
POCKET BOOKS, a division of Simon & Schuster Inc.
1230 Avenue of the Americas, New York, NY 10020

Copyright © 1995 by Parachute Press, Inc.

WHO'S BEEN SLEEPING IN MY GRAVE?
WRITTEN BY STEPHEN ROOS

ISBN: 0-671-52942-0

First Minstrel Books printing September 1995

10 9 8 7 6 5 4 3 2 1

FEAR STREET is a registered trademark of
Parachute Press, Inc.

A MINSTREL BOOK and colophon are registered trademarks
of Simon & Schuster Inc.

Cover art by Broeck Steadman

Printed in the U.S.A.

R·L·STINE'S

GHOSTS of FEAR STREET®

WHO'S BEEN SLEEPING
IN MY GRAVE?

Believe me, it isn't easy walking to school with your nose stuck in a book. In two blocks I had already tripped over a curb and bumped into a mailbox.

But I had to finish *Power Kids!*

"The sooner you read it, the sooner you'll be free from terror forever," the cover claimed. And if you know Shadyside, you know why I *needed* to finish the book—fast.

In regular towns you worry about regular things.

In Shadyside you worry about ghosts.

At least I do.

I'm scared of the ghost who wants to play hide-and-seek with kids in the Fear Street woods. I've never seen it myself. But I know people who have.

I'm scared of the burned-out Fear Street mansion. Ghosts have lived there for years and years. At least that's what my friends in school tell me.

And I have nightmares about Fear Street. It's the creepiest street in town—maybe in the whole world. Kevin, my fifteen-year-old brother, says the ghosts that haunt Fear Street are really evil. And horrible things will happen if they catch you.

I think Kevin is really evil. He loves trying to scare me.

But he won't be able to—not after I finish *Power Kids!* Nothing will scare me then. The book guarantees it—or I get my money back.

The kids in my class are going to be pretty upset. They love scaring me, too. Especially on Halloween—which is this Friday, only five days away.

Last Halloween they convinced me that a ghost salesman ran the shoe section in Dalby's Department Store. So I wore high-tops with huge holes in them all winter long. My toes froze.

Sometimes I imagine my friends keeping score. Whoever comes up with the story that scares me the most wins.

I hate it! But I'm almost a Power Kid now. So they'll have to find a new game this Halloween.

"Hey, Zack!" someone yelled.

I didn't bother to glance up from my book. It was Chris Hassler—one of my friends from school.

Chris and I are really different. Chris is short and chubby. He has bright red, curly hair and lots of freckles. Chris is usually laughing—or seems as if he's about to.

I do not look as if I'm about to burst out laughing. Big surprise, right? My grandmother says I have "very serious" eyes, like all the men in the Pepper family.

I have straight brown hair and I'm much taller than Chris. In fact, I'm the tallest kid in the fifth grade.

"Hey, Zack, wait up!" Chris called.

I kept my eyes glued to *Power Kids!* and walked faster.

Chris grabbed my arm as I hurried by his front gate. "Didn't you hear me?" he asked.

"Of course I heard you." I jerked my arm away. "I was trying to ignore you."

I crammed *Power Kids!* into my book bag as fast as I could. Chris would laugh his guts out if he spotted it.

3

"What are you hiding in there?" Chris demanded.

"Something my grandmother gave me for my birthday last week," I said.

"Your grandmother didn't give you any book! She gave you those polka-dot socks. I was at your party. Remember?"

"How could I forget?"

Chris grinned. "Come on. The snake I gave you was a cool present. I can't help it if you thought it was real. And you screamed your head off."

I reached into my backpack and pulled out the slimy rubber snake. "Well, it could have been real!" I shook it in his face.

Chris slapped the snake away. "If you hate it so much, how come you're carrying it around?"

"So I never forget how everyone laughed when I threw the box across the room," I explained. "Every time I see that snake, it will remind me not to let anyone scare me. Ever. Especially you." I returned the rubber snake to my backpack.

"Aw, come on, Zack," Chris whined. "Can't you take one little joke?"

"It's not one little joke," I insisted. "It's a lot of big jokes. Only they're not funny. They're mean!"

"It's not like I *tried* to be mean." Chris sounded hurt.

4

"Yeah, right." I snorted. "You thought I *wanted* to make a fool of myself at my own party."

"I'm sorry, Zack," he said quietly. "You're my best friend. And I really need to talk to you about something. Something serious."

"What?" I asked.

Chris slowly walked back toward his front door, his head down. He sat on the steps. I followed him.

"It's about a dog," Chris began. He talked so low I could hardly hear him. "I'm really worried about it."

"You're worried about a dog?" I said.

Chris peered left, then right. To see if anyone was listening. Then he whispered, "This isn't a regular dog. It's a ghost dog."

"A ghost dog!" I glared at Chris. "I know what you're trying to—"

"I'm not kidding this time," Chris interrupted. "I'm not. And I'm really scared."

Remember the snake, Zack, I told myself. Remember the snake. But then I noticed Chris's hands. They were trembling. Now I felt bad for being suspicious. "Okay," I said. "Tell me about it."

"Well, about a week ago we started hearing a dog howling in the middle of the night. We

5

searched for it. But we never found it. Then last night, my dad . . ." Chris hesitated.

"What?" I demanded.

"Last night my dad was taking the garbage out. And the ghost dog lunged for him." Chris swallowed hard.

"Why do you think it's a *ghost* dog?" I asked.

Chris inhaled deeply. "Dad used the garbage can lid to shield himself—but the dog jumped right through it.

Now my hands began to tremble.

"Wh-what does the ghost dog look like?" I stammered.

"It's pure white, with a big black spot on one side," Chris replied.

"Dad's sure the dog will be back tonight. And I'm really afraid."

Chris had barely finished his sentence when we heard it.

Howling.

I jerked my head up—and there it was. Coming right at me. A white dog. With a big black spot on its side.

The ghost dog!

2

The ghost dog growled. A mean growl. Then he leaped on top of me and knocked me down. The back of my head hit the top step with a thud.

A drop of the dog's hot saliva dripped down my neck.

I squeezed my eyes shut. I'm dead meat. Dead meat.

"Here, boy!" Chris yelled.

My eyes shot wide open. Chris stood over me, hugging the ghost dog.

"Gotcha!" he cried. "This is my cousin's dog. We're keeping him while my cousin's on vacation!"

I jumped up and grabbed my backpack off the porch. I couldn't think of anything rotten enough to call Chris Hassler. So I spun around and left.

"Zack!" Chris yelled. "You're not really mad, are you?"

I slammed the gate behind me. That's it, I ordered myself. No more falling for stupid ghost stories. Not from Chris. Not from my brother, Kevin. Not from anybody.

I hurried down the street. I noticed jack-o'-lanterns on some porches. And the big oak tree near the corner of Hawthorne Street had little strips of white sheets blowing from its branches.

This Halloween nothing is going to scare me. Nothing.

Chris raced after me. "How long are you going to hold a grudge this time?" he asked, panting.

"Go away," I snapped.

We turned the corner and I spotted the back of my best friend, Marcy Novi. She was headed toward school. Marcy sits in front of me in Miss Prescott's class. Which explains why I'm so good at recognizing her from the back.

I trotted up to her. Chris followed.

"Hi, guys," Marcy said. "Zack, what happened to your jacket?" She pointed to my sleeve.

8

I stared down. A jagged tear ran from my wrist to my elbow.

"Zack saved my life this morning," Chris answered before I could say anything. "He's a hero."

"Really?" Marcy asked, all excited.

"Yep," Chris said. "Zack rescued me from a ghost dog."

Marcy shook her head. "Another dumb joke, huh? And you fell for it, Zack?"

I shrugged.

Marcy doesn't make fun of people. That's one of the reasons she's my best friend. She's a good listener, too. I can really talk to her when something is bugging me.

The three of us hurried up the block and into school. As we reached Miss Prescott's class, the door flew open. Debbie Steinford burst into the hallway. Debbie's the shortest girl in the class. She tries to make up for it by having the biggest hair.

"Aren't you supposed to be going in the other direction?" Marcy asked. "The bell is about to ring."

Debbie shook her head. Her hair whipped my face. "We have a substitute teacher today. She wants new chalk from the supply closet."

"What happened to Miss Prescott?" I asked.

"I don't know," Debbie answered. "Sick, I guess."

Chris grinned. "A substitute. Cool. Let's all drop our books on the floor at nine-thirty. And then—"

"No way," I interrupted.

"But that's what substitutes are for," Chris said. "Don't be such a dweeb."

"Me? A dweeb? Do you think I'm a dweeb, Marcy?" I asked.

"Well, I can't picture you giving a substitute a hard time," Marcy said. "But that doesn't make you a dweeb."

"I bet even Chris will be nice to this sub." Debbie lowered her voice. "She's creepy."

"What do you mean?" I asked. I slid my hand into my backpack and touched the rubber snake. Careful, I told myself.

"I think she's a ghost, Zack," Debbie whispered.

"What's going on?" I demanded. "Is everyone trying to get a head start on Halloween—the official Scare Zack Day? Well, forget it. It's not working."

"But the substitute does look like a ghost," Debbie insisted, her eyes growing wide. "Her skin is so white, you can practically see through it. It's totally weird."

"Then I can't wait to get to class." I pushed past them. "Weird is what I like from now on."

I flung open the door to our classroom.

I choked back a scream.

Our new teacher *was* a ghost.

3

The substitute didn't have a face. Only two dark spots where her eyes should be. And she hovered above the floor.

I glanced around the classroom. Why didn't any of the other kids appear to be scared?

I focused on the substitute again. A veil! She's wearing a veil. That's why I thought she didn't have a face.

And she's not floating. She's wearing a fluffy white skirt that hangs to the floor. And white shoes.

And shiny white gloves. Nothing frightening about that. Strange, yes. Scary, no.

I took a deep breath and crossed the room to my desk. I felt pretty proud of myself. I had managed not to scream. And not to run away. I had remained calm and found the explanation.

Yes! I thought. I am a Power Kid.

I watched the substitute slowly reach up and remove her hat and veil. Her face was very wrinkled. And very pale. It was almost as white as her clothes. And it seemed sort of frozen.

Her scalp showed through her thin white hair. She must be a hundred years old, I thought.

Chris, Marcy, and Debbie entered the room as the bell rang.

"Good morning, boys and girls," the substitute began. "My name is Miss Gaunt. I'll be your teacher until Miss Prescott is feeling better. She's probably going to be out for the entire week. Perhaps in art class we can make a get-well card for her. Now please stand for the Pledge of Allegiance."

As soon as we finished the pledge, Miss Gaunt reached into the top drawer of the desk for Miss Prescott's attendance book.

"Abernathy, Danny," she called in a high, trembly voice.

"Here."

"Here?" she asked as she scanned the room.

"Just here? In my day young boys and girls always addressed their elders by name."

"Here, Miss Gaunt," Danny replied.

"Oh, that's much better, Danny," she said happily.

Miss Gaunt called more names. I noticed that she took the time to say something to each kid after she checked them off in the book.

"Hassler, Christopher."

"Here, Miss Gaunt," Chris called.

"What a good, clear voice you have, Chris," Miss Gaunt commented.

She continued to read out the names. I wonder what she'll say when she gets to me?

"Novi, Marcy."

"Here, Miss Gaunt," Marcy answered.

Miss Gaunt glanced up at Marcy. "What lovely hair you have, my dear."

"Thank you, Miss Gaunt."

"Pepper, Zachariah."

"Here, Miss Gaunt," I said.

"Zachariah. Such a lovely old-fashioned name." She closed her eyes and sighed.

"Everyone calls me Zack, Miss Gaunt," I told her. "Even my mom and dad."

"But you won't mind if I call you Zachariah,

will you?" she asked. "You'll be making an old woman very happy, you know."

I felt my ears turn hot. They always do that when I'm embarrassed.

"Sure," I mumbled.

Chris turned around in his seat, grinning at me. And mouthing one word over and over. I didn't have to be an expert lip-reader to know the word was *dweeb.*

When Miss Gaunt finished calling roll, she strolled up and down the aisles. She seemed to be studying us.

As she walked along the last row, next to the windows, a horrible squeaking sound filled the classroom. It made my teeth ache. What is that noise? I wondered.

I glanced over to the window ledge where Homer sits. Homer is our class hamster. He was running on his treadmill. I'd never seen him move so fast. The metal wheel squeaked louder and louder as he ran faster and faster.

What's wrong with him? I thought. We named Homer after Homer Simpson because he's such a couch potato. Walking to his food dish is his total exercise.

That's probably why the wheel is squeaking so much, I realized. It's never been used.

"My, what is he so excited about?" Miss Gaunt stared at Homer.

"Usually he sleeps all day," Marcy told her.

Miss Gaunt moved a few steps closer. She peered into Homer's cage. Homer ran even harder.

Miss Gaunt rapped playfully on the top of the cage.

"Good little hamster," she said softly. "You'll be quiet now, won't you?"

The squeaking sound stopped immediately. Homer jumped off the wheel and plopped down in the sawdust at the bottom of his cage.

Whoa, I thought. Miss Gaunt should open a hamster obedience school. Homer never does anything *I* tell him to.

"What do you children do after attendance?"

Chris's hand flew up. I knew what he was up to. But this time I planned to beat him to it.

I shot my hand up, too.

"Yes, Zachariah?"

"Right after attendance we have recess, Miss Gaunt," I announced. "And right after recess we go to lunch."

Most of the kids laughed. It will be a while before Chris calls me a dweeb again, I thought!

"Oh, I just love a boy with a sense of humor," Miss Gaunt said. "Tell me, Zachariah. Are you so amusing when you stay after school and write 'I Promise Never to Be a Smart Aleck' a hundred times on the blackboard?"

Miss Gaunt snatched up the pointer in the chalk tray. She walked toward my desk. When Chris played tricks on the substitutes, they never punished him. How come it backfired when I tried it?

"Zachariah, you didn't really mean to be so rude, did you?" Miss Gaunt asked. With each word she rapped the pointer on the top of my desk.

"No, Miss Gaunt," I mumbled, watching the pointer.

"I knew that," Miss Gaunt replied. "The moment I saw you, I just knew you were not that kind of boy."

"It's just that I—"

"Oh, you don't need to apologize. Not to me," she said. "You and I are going to get along fine."

Then she placed her fingers under my chin. Forcing me to stare up at her.

"I'll be keeping my eye on you, Zachariah Pepper!"

Even through her gloves, her touch was cold. Ice cold.

4

"Oh, Zach-a-ri-ah!" I heard Chris yell.

I spotted him and Marcy on the other side of the cafeteria. I wove around the long tables, then plopped down on the bench across from them. Chris leaned forward and made loud kissing noises. "Zach-a-ri-ah, such a bea-u-ti-ful name!" he cried in that clear voice Miss Gaunt liked so much.

"So what do you think of Miss Gaunt?" I asked, trying to ignore him.

"I think she needs to be arrested by the fashion police," Tiffany Loomis called from the corner of the table. "Where did she find those clothes?"

"Maybe she thought today was Halloween," Danny Abernathy volunteered.

"Yeah," Tiffany agreed. "But her clothes are even spookier than a Halloween costume."

"Did you notice how pale she is?" I asked. "I wonder if she ever goes out in the sun."

Marcy finished her sandwich. She stared off into space for a moment. Then she said, "Miss Gaunt is kind of strange, but she's really good at teaching things. Like that spelling trick about the word *weird:* '*Weird* is weird—it doesn't follow the *i* before *e* except after *c* rule.'"

"She is a pretty good teacher," I said. "But that's probably because she's been teaching forever. She must be a hundred years old."

"You know what I think about Miss Gaunt?" Chris asked. "I think she's in love with Zach-a-riah."

"Cut it out," I snapped back.

"She did pick you to feed Homer this week," Tiffany said, laughing.

I glanced up at the cafeteria clock. Ten minutes till lunch period ended. "I think I'll feed him now. I want to give him part of my apple."

"I'll come, too," Marcy said. "I have a piece of celery left.

19

"I'll help," Chris added. "But he's not getting any of my lunch."

The three of us grabbed our stuff and headed back to our classroom.

"Hello, children," Miss Gaunt called as we trooped in. "What eager students you are. Class doesn't begin for another ten minutes."

"We wanted to feed Homer his lunch," I explained.

"Very conscientious of you, Zachariah," she said.

"Thanks," I muttered. I waited for Chris to start laughing. He didn't. He was staring over my shoulder.

"Look!" he said, pointing. "Something terrible has happened to Homer!"

"Did the ghost dog get him?" I shot back. I couldn't believe Chris thought I'd fall for another one of his stupid jokes so soon.

"I'm not kidding!" Chris declared. "Something weird is going on!"

Marcy peered into Homer's cage. "Chris is right!"

I turned around and stared at the hamster.

Every single hair on Homer's body had turned white.

5

All the kids returned from lunch. We huddled around Homer's cage.

"Maybe someone switched hamsters on us," Chris said. "Maybe it *isn't* Homer."

"Oh, it's Homer, all right," Marcy insisted. "Look at his ear. See the little rip in it? Remember when he had the accident? It's still Homer."

"I've heard of this happening to people if something really scary happens to them," I said. "I didn't know it could happen to animals, too."

But it did happen. And I knew who was to blame.

Miss Gaunt.

I remembered how strange Homer acted this morning when she stood near his cage. She must have something to do with this, I thought. She must.

"What's going on here?" Miss Gaunt asked, coming up behind us.

"Homer turned white," Chris explained, stepping back from the cage so Miss Gaunt could see.

The minute Homer spotted Miss Gaunt, his entire body began to shake. And he burrowed his head under some sawdust.

He's trembling, I noticed. Animals are supposed to be good judges of people. And Homer is terrified. Anyone can see that.

Uh-oh, I thought. What if Miss Gaunt really is—a ghost!

"Turning white is not that unusual," Miss Gaunt said, interrupting my thoughts. "Many animals turn white as winter comes. It's their camouflage."

"You mean it protects them from being eaten by other animals?" Danny asked.

Miss Gaunt smiled at him. "Very good, Danny," she said. "It is much more difficult to see a white animal against white snow. And more difficult to see means more difficult to catch—and eat."

"Does anyone know of another animal that changes color in the winter?"

"An ermine?" Marcy called out.

"Well done, Marcy," Miss Gaunt said. "Or it is possible that Homer has a vitamin deficiency. That can often make an animal's fur change color. Perhaps we can ask your science teacher."

When I thought about it, Miss Gaunt's explanations made sense. "Oh, boy. I almost did it again," I muttered. "I almost freaked out over nothing. I have to finish *Power Kids!* tonight."

Miss Gaunt clapped her hands. "Finish feeding Homer, children. We have work to do."

I pulled out the hamster's water bottle and filled it in the sink in the back of the room. Miss Gaunt followed me.

"You seemed very interested in my little science lesson, Zachariah."

I didn't know what to say. I spied Chris staring at us. His mouth curled up in his stupid grin.

Miss Gaunt didn't wait for an answer. "I enjoy teaching so much more when I have an enthusiastic student," she told me.

I nodded quickly and hurried back to Homer's

cage with the bottle. On the way I passed Chris's seat. "Here comes the teacher's pet," he whispered to Tiffany. She giggled.

By the time I returned to my desk, Miss Gaunt had started the history lesson. "This afternoon we will continue your study of the American Revolution," she announced. She opened a box and dumped a bunch of old metal soldiers on her desk.

"Danny, I would like you to lead the British," she instructed. "Come collect your soldiers."

As Danny headed toward the front of the room, Miss Gaunt asked, "Who would like to take the role of George Washington?" Lots of kids raised their hands. Her eyes searched the room.

I stared down at my desk. The soldiers looked like fun, but I didn't want to get chosen for anything. Not by her.

"Zachariah, would you lead the rebel forces?" she called.

I heard Chris snicker.

I shuffled up to Miss Gaunt's desk and gathered up a handful of soldiers.

That's when I noticed something on the side of Miss Gaunt's neck. A deep purple blotch. Kind of long and bumpy.

I didn't want Miss Gaunt to notice me staring. I

24

glanced down at my soldiers. Then I stole another quick peek.

The thing on Miss Gaunt's neck moved.

It was alive!

Miss Gaunt had a fat, slimy worm crawling on her neck!

6

The worm was thick and wet looking. I watched as Miss Gaunt reached up and picked it off her neck. Then she squooshed it between her gloved fingers and tossed it into the wastebasket.

I glanced at the other kids. They were all gathered around a huge map Miss Gaunt had spread on the floor. No one had noticed a thing.

Maybe it was a piece of fuzz, I tried to convince myself. But I didn't think so.

I didn't talk to anybody the rest of the afternoon. After history we made a card for Miss Prescott. Then it was time to go home.

Marcy, Chris, and I left school together. But I

didn't say anything to them about what I had seen.

That night I made sure I finished reading *Power Kids!*

Okay, Zack, I told myself as I opened the classroom door the next morning, it's power time. You did *not* see a worm on Miss Gaunt's neck yesterday. Remember what *Power Kids!* said: You see what you expect to see.

And you always expect to see something scary, I reminded myself.

But not anymore!

I calmly walked over to my desk and sat down. I studied Miss Gaunt's neck carefully. Pasty white skin. Nothing else. No worm.

Miss Gaunt took the attendance and I began to relax. We said the Pledge of Allegiance.

Then we began a math lesson. "Who would like to go to the blackboard and show the class how to multiply decimals?" Miss Gaunt asked.

I tried to make myself invisible. I scrunched down in my chair. I was safe. Lots of kids waved their hands.

"How about you showing us, Zachariah?" Miss Gaunt suggested.

"Actually, I'm not all that good at decimals, Miss Gaunt," I admitted.

27

"That's why we come to school, isn't it?" Miss Gaunt asked. "So we can learn to do better?"

"But you see, I'm not—" I began, but my mouth grew dry. My voice cracked.

"Not feeling well, dear?" Miss Gaunt asked in her high little voice. "You're not coming down with a sore throat, are you?" She walked down the aisle toward me. "Do you need to see the school nurse?"

She reached out to press her hand on my forehead.

"Honest, Miss Gaunt," I said, pulling away. "I'm fine." I didn't want to feel the touch of her icy fingers again.

Miss Gaunt stretched out her hand once more. Her white glove smelled a little like dirt. And it looked grimy.

As she placed her hand on my forehead, I remembered how cold my grandmother's hands were sometimes. Grandma said it was because of poor circulation—it happens when people get older.

I forced myself to sit still. Miss Gaunt couldn't help that her hands were cold.

But when she touched me, I felt the cold all the way inside my head. A sharp stinging pain.

"Well, you don't have a fever, Zachariah," Miss

Gaunt said. "Could it be that you're afraid of making a mistake—and the other children teasing you?"

I shrugged. "I don't understand decimals at all."

"Well, no one's going to laugh at you, Zachariah. Not in my classroom. Besides, I never met a Zachariah who didn't multiply decimals beautifully!"

I glanced around the room. None of the kids seemed as if they were about to laugh. Not even Chris. But even if they didn't laugh now, I knew they'd make fun of me after school.

But I had no choice. I approached the chalkboard.

"Thirty-seven point twenty-nine multiplied by four hundred and seventy-two point sixty-three," Miss Gaunt instructed. "Write it on the blackboard, Zachariah."

My hand trembled. I could barely write out the numbers.

"Go ahead," she said. "Now write down the answer."

I swallowed hard. "I can't," I said quietly.

"Why is that, Zachariah?" Miss Gaunt asked.

"Because I don't know how." Is Miss Gaunt going to make me stand up here all day? I was beginning to panic. I felt my ears turn hot.

"You can do it, Zachariah," Miss Gaunt said firmly. "I know you can, dear."

She stepped toward me.

Squeak. Squeak. Squeak. I heard Homer in his cage. Running wildly on his treadmill again.

"Be still, Homer," Miss Gaunt called. "Let Zachariah concentrate now."

The squeaking stopped abruptly.

My hand floated into the air. I squeezed the chalk between my fingers, but I didn't feel anything. My fingers were numb.

What's happening? It felt as though a big magnet was tugging my hand up. Up to the chalkboard.

Then I began to write. My hand wrote number after number.

"Very good, Zachariah," Miss Gaunt said proudly. "I knew you could do it."

But I knew I didn't do it. Something else did. Something else had control of my arm!

7

My arm flopped back to my side. The chalk flew from my fingers. It broke against the floor.

"Well done, Zachariah," Miss Gaunt said. "You may return to your seat."

I stumbled down the aisle to my desk and slid into the chair. My arm felt itchy. Prickly.

I stared down at my hand and wiggled my fingers.

I raised my eyes to Miss Gaunt. She smiled at me proudly—and winked.

She did it, I thought. Miss Gaunt forced me to write the correct answer. She moved my hand!

Power Kids! didn't cover anything like this. I

had to tell Marcy and Chris. This wasn't my imagination. This was for real.

When the lunch bell finally rang, I bolted out the door. I waited a few feet down the hall for Marcy and Chris.

"You did great in math," Marcy called when she spotted me.

"Yeah," Chris agreed.

"It wasn't me," I told them.

"What do you mean?" Chris asked.

I motioned for them to move away from the door. I didn't want Miss Gaunt—or anyone else—to hear what I had to say.

"It wasn't me," I repeated. "I didn't know the answers, and I didn't move my hand."

"What?" Chris demanded.

"Miss Gaunt took control of me. She made my hand move," I whispered. "She's a ghost. I know it."

Chris clutched his chest and staggered back a few steps. "No!" he cried. Then he started to laugh.

"Come on, Zack," Marcy pleaded.

"Think about it," I insisted. "Homer turned white on the day she started. Your hair turns white when you get scared, right?"

"My mother said her hair turned white the day she had me," Chris joked.

Marcy ignored him. "Miss Gaunt explained about Homer turning white, remember? Camouflage or vitamin deficiency."

"But other strange things have happened, too," I insisted.

"Yeah," Chris chimed in. "Don't forget—Zack got the right answer to a decimal question!"

Marcy slapped Chris on the shoulder.

"He's right, Marcy. I didn't know the answer. I'm telling you—she moved my hand! And there's something else," I said. "I saw a worm on Miss Gaunt's neck yesterday, and it didn't even bother her. She just squooshed it."

"Gross!" Marcy exclaimed.

"Cool," Chris added.

"So what are we going to do about Miss Gaunt?" I asked.

"Bring her some Worms-Away?" Chris suggested. "That's what we give my cousin's dog."

I didn't really expect any help from Chris. But what would Marcy say?

Marcy shook her head. "She *is* really creepy, Zack. But she's not a ghost. There's no such thing as ghosts."

Not even Marcy—my best friend—believed me. What was I going to do?

Marcy grabbed my arm and pulled me down the hall. "Let's go eat. Maybe you'll feel better after lunch."

"I'm so hungry I could eat a ghost horse," Chris said as he followed us to the cafeteria.

I stopped suddenly.

"What's wrong?" Marcy asked.

"Nothing. I left my lunch in my desk. I'll meet you guys inside."

I dashed down the hall. If Miss Gaunt is still in the classroom, I'll skip lunch, I thought. Because I'm definitely not going in there alone.

I peeked inside. The room was empty.

I hurried to my desk and opened the top.

Something white fluttered to the ground.

It was one of Miss Gaunt's gloves!

8

Why was Miss Gaunt's glove in my desk? I wondered. She must have been snooping around, I guessed. And dropped it there by accident.

I didn't say anything about the glove to Marcy or Chris during lunch. In fact, I didn't say much of anything. I didn't really feel like talking.

After lunch we piled into the classroom. Chris's hand shot up before Miss Gaunt could say a word.

Oh, no. I stiffened in my seat. He's going to tell everyone what I said. He's going to tell them Miss Gaunt is a ghost.

"Miss Gaunt," Chris began. "Halloween is coming up—"

I sank down. And let out a long sigh.

"And Miss Prescott said we could have a party on Friday," Chris announced.

"Then we shall have one," Miss Gaunt told him. "Thank you for bringing it up, Chris."

Miss Gaunt turned to the chalkboard. "Let's begin with a list of what we need."

"Cookies," Debbie called out.

Miss Gaunt started to write on the board. The chalk snapped and fell from her fingers. Bobby Dreyfuss picked it up for her. He sat in the front row.

I could hardly read the words she wrote. The letters were all different sizes. And very wobbly.

"Decorations," Marcy suggested.

The chalk screeched across the board as Miss Gaunt continued the list. She dropped the chalk again.

"Is something wrong with your hand?" Bobby asked as he picked up the chalk again and handed it to Miss Gaunt.

"It's just a little arthritis," Miss Gaunt said. "It happens when we get older."

"Do you have arthritis in your other hand, too, Miss Gaunt?" Bobby asked.

I noticed that Miss Gaunt held her right hand tucked inside her blouse. Doesn't she usually write with that hand? I thought she did, but I couldn't remember.

"Why don't we keep our attention on what we need for the party," Miss Gaunt suggested.

"But I only—" Bobby started.

"Please, Bobby," Miss Gaunt said stiffly. "Let's go on with the list."

Miss Gaunt dropped the chalk in the tray. "Perhaps we don't need a list. Debbie, would you like to volunteer for the liquid refreshment?" she asked.

"You mean drinks?" Debbie asked uncertainly.

"Exactly, dear," Miss Gaunt replied. "People enjoy cider at Halloween parties. Do you think you could manage that?"

"Yes, Miss Gaunt," Debbie said.

"How about cups and plates?"

Danny waved his hand in the air. "My dad works over at Dalby's," he told her. "He can get them for us free, I bet."

"Why, how nice," Miss Gaunt said. "Will you thank your father for us?"

"Can we play games?" Chris asked. "We've been collecting money to buy some."

"What kinds of games did you have in mind, Chris?" Miss Gaunt asked. "Something like Pin the Tail on the Donkey?"

"More like Pin the Fangs on the Werewolf," Chris said. "Or how about Dead Man's Bluff?"

"That sounds a bit frightening, doesn't it?" Miss Gaunt asked. "Do you children really enjoy these games?"

"It's Halloween," Chris insisted. "It's supposed to be scary. I bet we could find some cool games down at Dalby's."

"Why don't you try Shop Till You Drop," Miss Gaunt said. "It's a new place over by the Stop 'N' Shop. Take Zack and Marcy with you. They can help pick out decorations there. But nothing too horrifying, please."

The last bell rang. I leaped out of my chair and headed for the door.

"Would you stay behind, Zachariah?" Miss Gaunt called.

"Just me?" I asked.

"Don't worry," she said. "I only want to ask you a little question, dear."

Miss Gaunt waited until everyone left the classroom. Then she closed the door and turned toward me.

"May I have it?" she asked.

"Have *what,* Miss Gaunt?"

"You have something that belongs to me, Zachariah," she stated.

38

"I didn't take anything," I said. "Honest."

"But I saw you put it in your pocket, dear," she said. "It should still be there."

I stuck my hand into my pocket. Her glove. I forgot that I shoved it in there.

I pulled the glove out. It slipped from my fingers and fluttered to the floor.

"Do you think you could pick that up for me, Zachariah?" Miss Gaunt asked.

As I bent over I said, "I'm sorry about your arthritis, Miss Gaunt." Then I held the glove out to her.

"What arthritis, dear?"

"But you told Bobby—"

"Oh, Bobby is so nosy," Miss Gaunt declared. "I had to tell him something, didn't I?"

She reached for the glove with her left hand. Then she whipped her right hand out from the fold of her blouse.

And there wasn't any skin on her fingers!

Only bones.

The bones of a skeleton.

9

"Her hand—it was horrible," I told Chris and Marcy. "It didn't have any skin on it."

My knees began to buckle as I described it.

We were on our way to the party decoration store—the one Miss Gaunt told us about.

"And we shouldn't go to this store," I added. "We shouldn't do anything Miss Gaunt tells us to do."

"Get a grip," Chris said.

"How long did you see her hand for, anyway?"

"Just for a second," I admitted. "Until she put her glove back on. But that was long enough. I'm telling you—Miss Gaunt is a ghost."

"Come on, Zack. That's what happens when people grow old," Marcy explained. "They get very thin."

"It wasn't just thin," I insisted. "It was bony—like a real skeleton's hand!"

"Look! There it is," Chris said, pointing. "The party store."

I gazed across the street. There it was, all right. Miss Gaunt said its name was Shop Till You Drop. But the sign out front read Shop Till You Drop *Dead.*

"Oooooo. There could be ghosts inside, Zack!" Chris joked when he noticed the sign. "Are you sure you want to go in?"

"Don't be an idiot, Chris," Marcy replied, crossing the street.

"I don't think it's open," I said as we neared the store. "I don't see any lights on."

Marcy was the first to reach the front door. "Oh, I get it," she said. "Someone's painted the windows black." She pressed her face against the glass. She cupped her hands around her eyes. "I can't see anything in there."

She pushed on the door. It opened silently.

Inside a single dirty bulb hung from the ceiling. It swung back and forth, back and forth—casting creepy shadows on the walls.

The store appeared to be huge—but it was hard to tell in the dim light. It also appeared to be empty.

"Hello! Is anybody here?" Chris yelled. No one answered.

The door banged shut behind us.

"Anybody here?" Chris called again.

I heard a soft rustling sound. Then silence.

My eyes adjusted to the darkness. The store was lined with tall wooden shelves that stretched almost to the ceiling. Beyond them, the back of the store was bathed in a deep purple glow.

"Let's go to Dalby's," Marcy said. "This place *is* creepy."

"Yeah," I agreed.

"I want to stay," Chris argued. "I bet we can find some cool Halloween stuff here. Besides, I promised my mom I'd be home by four. I don't have time to go to another place."

Chris hurried down one of the narrow aisles.

I followed him. I didn't want him telling everyone in school that I freaked out in a Halloween store.

Everything smelled strange. Kind of moldy—like old mushrooms. And the floor felt bumpy and uneven. I heard something crunch under my feet.

"How are we supposed to find anything when

we can't *see* anything?" Marcy muttered behind me.

We took a few more steps.

Crunch, crunch, crunch.

"What is making that noise?" Marcy asked.

I stared down at the floor. "I can't tell," I answered. "It sounds like we're walking on peanut shells or something."

I crouched down, peered at my shoes—and saw them. Millions of them.

Millions of slimy black beetles swarming all over the floor.

Marcy spotted them, too. We both gasped.

Suddenly a bright overhead light flashed on. Marcy kneeled to study the beetles. Then she picked one up!

"Plastic," she announced. "Plastic bugs."

"Uh, I guess they decorated the whole store for Halloween," I said. "Pretty cool, huh?"

We both laughed.

"Hey, Marcy, the light that went on—who threw the switch?" I asked. We both glanced around. No one was in sight.

"Where's Chris?" Marcy asked.

"He was right in front of me a minute ago," I told her.

I figured Chris was probably hiding down one of

43

the aisles. Waiting to jump out at us. Well, he's not going to get me this time, I told myself. I scanned the shelves, searching for something creepy to use to scare him first.

The shelves were crammed with all kinds of strange stuff. A jar full of glass eyeballs. A withered hand. A mesh bag filled with small bones. And some cool masks.

I grabbed two masks. I pulled a gorilla mask over my head. It smelled rotten inside—like spoiled meat. But I didn't care.

I handed the other mask to Marcy. It was really gross. A monster face with one eyeball hanging from a bloody thread.

"Chris!" I shouted as loud as I could. "Where are you?"

Then I leaned in close to Marcy and whispered, "I bet Chris is hiding around that corner. Let's scare him before he can scare us."

Marcy smiled and slipped the mask over her head.

We tiptoed to the end of the aisle. I hope Chris doesn't hear those stupid plastic bugs crunching, I thought.

I turned to Marcy and held up three fingers. She nodded. We'd both jump around the corner on the count of three.

I gave the signal and leaped out. I beat on my chest and howled.

Marcy screeched—high and long. I was impressed. She really sounded scary.

Someone *was* standing around that corner, but it wasn't Chris. It was a man. The strangest man I had ever seen. His head was big and round—the size of a basketball. The pasty skin on his face stretched right up over his bald scalp. He wore a shiny black cape that trailed to the floor.

Marcy dug her fingernails into my arm and pointed—to something lying on the ground at the man's feet.

It was Chris. Lying absolutely still.

A trickle of blood ran from the corner of his mouth.

10

"**W**hat did you do to Chris!" I screamed. Marcy and I ripped off our masks and fell to Chris's side.

"Chris!" Marcy cried. "Chris, are you okay?"

Chris's eyes fluttered. He struggled to sit up. Then he cried, "Gotcha!"

Marcy and I glared at him.

"Come on, guys. Say something," Chris whined. "Hey, don't you think this fake blood is great?"

"Yes, it is delicious, isn't it?" the bald man replied.

Chris jerked his head back. "Who are you?" he asked, scrambling to his feet.

"I?" the man asked. "Why, I am Mr. Sangfwad.

The owner of this establishment. How may I serve you?" He stroked the head of a small, furry animal buried in his arms.

"We're here for Halloween," Chris mumbled.

"To buy games and decorations for our class party," Marcy added.

"Oh, oh, oh!" Mr. Sangfwad exclaimed. "Evangeline must have sent you!" Then he grinned, showing off a big dark hole where his two front teeth used to be.

"Evangeline?" Chris asked.

"From Shadyside Middle School," Mr. Sangfwad explained. "The substitute teacher."

"Oh!" I groaned. "You must mean Miss Gaunt."

"Yes. Yes. Miss Gaunt. And you must be Zachariah," Mr. Sangfwad said, studying me carefully. "Evangeline speaks very highly of you."

"Do you really know Miss Gaunt?" I asked.

"Why, of course I do. Miss Gaunt and I have been friends in Shadyside forever. Haven't we, Phoebe?" he crooned to the little gray pet in his arms.

"But I've lived here my whole life," I said. "I've never seen either of you before."

"Life is strange, isn't it?" Mr. Sangfwad replied.

47

That wasn't exactly the answer I was looking for.

With both hands Mr. Sangfwad lifted his pet high in the air.

Its tiny black eyes popped into view.

Then its whiskers.

Then its sharp yellow teeth.

A rat!

"You're holding a rat!" I cried.

"Oh, don't let Phoebe scare you." Mr. Sangfwad kissed the top of the rat's head. "She's quite sweet."

"She could bite you!" Chris warned.

"Rats will be rats," Mr. Sangfwad said.

"You could die!" Marcy exclaimed.

"I said she was sweet," Mr. Sangfwad replied. "I didn't say she was harmless!"

Mr. Sangfwad placed Phoebe on the floor. I hoped she would scurry away. But instead she circled our feet.

"Now. Exactly what kind of games would you like for your Halloween party?" Mr. Sangfwad asked.

"Do you have Pin the Fangs on the Werewolf and Dead Man's Bluff?" Chris asked.

"Why, of course," Mr. Sangfwad answered. "They are in aisle three, and—" Chris headed

48

over to the aisle before Mr. Sangfwad finished. "Don't forget Spin the Zombie and Power Ghouls," he called after him.

"Do you have Halloween decorations?" Marcy asked politely.

"Halloween decorations? For Evangeline's students? Of course I do. I suppose you want black and orange streamers—that sort of thing."

"Exactly," I told him. I couldn't wait to leave the store. Mr. Sangfwad gave me the creeps.

When we had everything we needed, Marcy and I met Chris at the cash register.

Mr. Sangfwad rang up the order. Marcy paid him with the money we had collected in school.

"I'm afraid I've run out of bags," Mr. Sangfwad announced, searching under the counter. "I have some in back if you would wait just a moment."

Chris checked his watch. "It's ten to four. I've gotta go. My mom will kill me if I'm not home on time today."

"Go ahead," Marcy told him. "Zack and I can handle this stuff."

"Great." Chris hurried out the front door. "See ya!"

Marcy and I waited by the cash register. I shifted from one foot to the other. I wanted to get out of there.

"What's taking him so long?" I complained.

"He just left," Marcy said. "Be patient."

I kept checking my watch. "Maybe we can carry this stuff without bags," I suggested. "We've already paid. Let's go."

"Shhh," Marcy whispered. "Here he comes."

"Okeydokey," Mr. Sangfwad sang out cheerfully, approaching the counter. He piled all our decorations into a bag.

"Now, are you sure you have everything you need for your party?" he asked. "Halloween is very, very important to Evangeline."

Then he stared directly into my eyes and added, "I know *you* wouldn't want to disappoint her."

"Well?" I demanded once we stepped outside. Do you believe me now?"

"Do I believe what?" Marcy asked.

"That Miss Gaunt is a ghost," I shot back.

"Zack, you're being ridiculous."

"How can you say that?" I practically shrieked. "Everything about her is totally weird—including her creepy friend Mr. Sangfwad and his horrible store."

"Mr. Sangfwad was kind of strange...." Marcy's voice trailed off.

"Kind of strange?" I screeched. "He had a rat for a pet! And didn't you hear what he said—that

he and Miss Gaunt have lived in Shadyside *forever?*"

"So, what's your point?" Marcy asked.

"Don't you think it's kind of funny that we've never seen either of them before?"

"Well . . ." Marcy began.

"Come with me after school tomorrow," I interrupted. "I'm going to follow Miss Gaunt. And I'm going to get real proof."

"Fine," Marcy said.

"Then—you mean—you believe me?" I asked excitedly.

"No," Marcy replied. "I'm going with you to prove once and for all that there are no such things as ghosts!"

"She *is* a ghost, Marcy. You'll see!"

Was I right? Was Miss Gaunt really a ghost?

I wasn't sure of anything anymore.

But we were going to follow her. And we were finally going to find out.

I had no idea what my decision would lead to.

12

The next morning we rode our bikes to school. We'd use them afterward to follow Miss Gaunt.

I couldn't wait for the final bell to ring. But by the end of the day, I began to feel scared. What if Miss Gaunt caught us following her?

Even if she wasn't a ghost, she'd be pretty angry. And we'd be in tons of trouble.

If she was a ghost, things could be a lot worse.

What did ghosts do to people who stumbled in their way?

I didn't know. And I didn't want to find out.

After the last bell rang, Marcy and I hid alongside the school trophy case in the front hall. We watched all the kids leave.

Then Miss Gaunt appeared. She approached the school's two heavy steel front doors. I noticed how tiny and frail she seemed in front of them. I wondered if she would have trouble opening them. I always do. But when she grabbed the exit bar and pushed, the door flew open.

"Did you see that?" I whispered to Marcy. "Did you see how easily she opened the door? Now what do you think?"

Marcy stared at me—as if I were nuts.

No sense in starting an argument with her, I decided. We would both find out the truth soon enough.

When the door swung closed, we crept over to it. We opened it a crack and watched Miss Gaunt climb down the steps.

She headed across the school yard. Then she ducked behind some bushes. We dashed outside.

"Oh, no!" I cried. "We've lost her already!"

"No, we haven't," Marcy said, jabbing me in the ribs.

She was right. There was Miss Gaunt—out from behind the bushes. Pedaling a bike!

"I can't believe Miss Gaunt rides a bike," I said as we ran over to ours. "She's too old for that."

We leaped on our bikes and charged after her.

By the time we reached the first intersection, Miss Gaunt had disappeared.

"Do you think she turned left or right on Park Drive?" Marcy asked.

"I don't know. We'll just have to guess."

The light turned green, and we turned right on Park. There was Miss Gaunt—directly ahead of us. "Yes!" I cried.

Miss Gaunt turned right again. Onto Fear Street.

I remembered what my brother, Kevin, told me about Fear Street—that the most evil ghosts of all haunted it.

"It figures," I moaned to Marcy. "Miss Gaunt lives on Fear Street."

"Even if she does live on Fear Street, that doesn't mean she's a ghost," Marcy said firmly.

We rode by the houses on Fear Street. Some of them were all fixed up. A lot of them were wrecks, with sagging porches and peeling paint.

And some were totally abandoned. Looming above all of them was the burned-out shell of the Fear mansion. That one was definitely the scariest.

We pedaled quickly by the mansion. Following Miss Gaunt around one curve after another.

The afternoon sun was beginning to set. Fear Street was really spooky in the dark. And we didn't see a single car going in either direction. No joggers. No other bikes. No people out for a stroll.

My head began to throb. It was too scary here. I wanted to turn around and go home.

I was about to suggest it, but Marcy spoke first. "Look! She's slowing down."

"I bet we're coming to her house!" I exclaimed.

I watched Miss Gaunt slip off her bike.

She leaned it against two huge iron gates.

The gates of the Fear Street Cemetery!

13

I slowly reached out and pushed open the iron gate. It felt as cold as Miss Gaunt's fingers.

I glanced over at Marcy. I could tell she was waiting for me to go in first. "So what do you think now?" I asked her.

"People visit graveyards, you know," Marcy replied. But I thought I heard a little quiver in her voice.

I slipped through the gate, Marcy right behind me. I felt like an intruder. The stone angels seemed to stare down at me disapprovingly.

We ran from grave to grave. Ducking behind each tombstone before we sprinted to the next. We had to be very careful. We definitely did not want Miss Gaunt to spot us.

A sudden gust of wind set the autumn leaves swirling. Swirling around the tombstones.

The last rays of the sun had faded. And I shivered in the blast of chilly air.

Miss Gaunt glided between the graves. Marcy and I followed.

"Zack," Marcy whispered, pointing to the ground. "Look!"

I glanced down. A whirling gray mist covered our feet. "Hey! Where did that come from?"

The mist slowly rose to our knees. We watched as it grew thicker. And higher.

"Maybe we should head back," I said anxiously. Then I changed my mind. "No, we can't. We've got to follow Miss Gaunt!"

But when I gazed up, Miss Gaunt had disappeared!

"Where did she go?" I cried.

"I don't know," Marcy replied, squinting to see through the churning gray spray. "The mist is too thick. I think we should go back."

"Okay. Okay," I agreed. "But which way is back?"

"Just follow me," Marcy replied. Then she broke into a run, dashing between the gravestones.

58

"Slow down, Marcy!" I cried out, trying to keep up.

Marcy tripped over something—probably a rock. I couldn't tell. The mist covered everything now. She hit the ground with a soft thud. But in a second she was up again, running faster.

"Marcy!" I cried out. "Slow down. I'm going to lose you."

Marcy stumbled once more.

I spotted her arms waving frantically through the mist.

"Zack!" she screamed. "Help me!"

Then she sank totally out of sight.

I waited. Waited for her to jump up—so I would know which way to go.

But Marcy didn't appear.

"Marcy!" I yelled. "Where are you?"

Marcy had vanished.

14

"**M**arcy!" I called out, louder this time. "Marcy!"

No answer.

I inched forward.

The mist swirled all around me now. It was impossible to see.

Where was Marcy? Had she run into Miss Gaunt? Did Miss Gaunt have her trapped right now?

My heart hammered away in my chest. The mist had grown icy, and I began to shiver. But I pressed on, calling Marcy's name out every few steps.

"Marcy! Where are you? Marcy!"

"Over here, Zack!"

Marcy!

I stepped in the direction of her voice—and my legs flew out from under me.

I plunged down—down into total darkness.

And then, finally, I landed—somewhere damp and very, very dark.

"Oooh," I groaned, rubbing my head.

As I fumbled to sit up, a cold hand groped in the darkness and grabbed my arm.

"Let me go!" I screamed, trying desperately to shake loose.

"Zack! Stop it! It's me."

"Marcy!" I cried with relief. "Where are we?"

"I think we've fallen into a grave."

"A grave? Oh, gross!" I shouted. "Are we—are we alone down here?"

"Of course we're alone down here," Marcy snapped. "That's why we fell. We fell into an empty grave."

"Okay. Okay," I said. "I just thought that . . . maybe . . . Miss Gaunt was down here, too."

"Zack, she was headed in the other direction when we lost her."

"Oh. Right," I said.

Marcy sighed.

"It's really disgusting down here," I said, glancing around the underground pit. "How are we going to get out?"

"Good question," Marcy replied.

I stood up. Then Marcy and I tried to fling ourselves out of the grave.

But the walls were too high.

We searched the sides of the grave for a rock, a tree root, something to grab on to—to hoist ourselves up. But the dirt simply slipped through our fingers.

"Hey, I have an idea," I said to Marcy. "Give me a boost. Once I'm out, I can help pull you up."

Marcy knit her hands together. I slipped my foot into them and pushed off with all my might. My hands flew up and found the grave opening.

"I'm out!" I shouted.

I hung from the grave's edge, my feet dangling below. Marcy shoved my legs up as I pulled myself to the ground above.

Then I leaned over and dragged Marcy up.

Marcy tumbled out, and we both toppled backward onto the ground.

"Oh, no," Marcy moaned.

"Are you hurt?" I asked.

Marcy didn't answer my question. She simply

stared ahead. And even in the dark I could see she was trembling. Finally she said,

"Read it, Zack."

Marcy was staring at a gravestone. The gravestone at the head of the empty grave.

It was very old.

I could barely make out the engraving.

I moved up close to it, squinted, and read:

EVANGELINE GAUNT
BORN 1769   DIED 1845
REST IN PEACE

"It's *her* grave!" I screamed. "We were in *her* grave!"

15

"She *is* a ghost!" I cried. "Let's get out of here. Before she finds us!"

We charged through the cemetery, stumbling over rocks and dodging graves.

We ran and ran. But we were nowhere near the entrance.

"It's a maze!" Marcy cried. "We're going around in circles."

I stopped. My eyes darted left and right. Trying to find a clue to guide us.

The mist began to lift, and I spotted some hedges a few feet away. "Let's go through there!" I cried.

I parted the hedges and held them back so Marcy could squeeze through. The little thorns ripped into my hands. But I didn't care.

As I shoved through the hedge after Marcy, I yelled, "Look! The entrance! We're almost there!"

We dashed to the gates, jumped on our bikes, and pedaled as hard as we could. We didn't speak until we reached Marcy's house.

"*Now* do you believe me?"

Marcy nodded, gasping for breath. "Miss Gaunt is a ghost. What are we going to do?"

I wiped the sweat from my forehead. "We have to tell the rest of the kids as soon as we reach school tomorrow," I said. "Meet me outside the main entrance at eight-fifteen. We'll catch them before they go in—and warn them. . . ."

I paced back and forth the next morning in front of the school. I glanced at my watch for the hundreth time—8:25 . . . 8:27 . . . 8:31 . . .

Not it was 8:45 and still no Marcy.

Where could she be? I wondered. Most of the kids had arrived and gone inside.

I didn't stop them.

I didn't want to tell them about Miss Gaunt alone. I told Marcy we would do it together.

65

Besides, I knew no one would believe *me*. I needed Marcy there.

I glanced at my watch one last time—9:00.

I had to go in.

But now I was worried—really worried about Marcy.

Where was she?

Did Miss Gaunt see us yesterday?

Did she know we were following her?

Did she find Marcy this morning and do something horrible to her?

I bolted through the classroom door just as Miss Gaunt began taking attendance. I shot a glance at Marcy's seat. It was empty.

"Abernathy, Danny."

"Here, Miss Gaunt."

I studied Miss Gaunt as she called roll. Her high little voice sounded the same as always. She didn't seem upset—or angry.

"Hassler, Chris."

"Here, Miss Gaunt."

I wondered if Miss Gaunt could tell how upset *I* was.

I held my breath until Miss Gaunt reached Marcy's name.

"Novi, Marcy."

No answer.

"Can anyone tell me why Marcy Novi is not here this morning?" she asked.

No one volunteered.

"Oh, I just remembered," Miss Gaunt said. "Marcy's out for a few days, I'm afraid."

"Is she sick, Miss Gaunt?" Tiffany asked. "Should we send her a card?"

"I doubt it would reach her in time," Miss Gaunt said.

"In time for what?" Tiffany asked.

In time for what?

Suddenly my hands began to shake.

"Really, Tiffany," Miss Gaunt replied. "Would you like to hear someone telling the whole class your family secrets?"

"It's a *secret?*" Tiffany asked excitedly.

Miss Gaunt shook her head in disapproval. Then she continued on.

"Reynolds," she called out sharply.

"Here, Miss Gaunt!"

"Steinford."

"Here, Miss Gaunt!"

Marcy was in trouble. I have to find her, I thought. And fast!

I didn't hear a word Miss Gaunt said all morning. All I could think about was Marcy. I couldn't wait for the lunch bell to ring.

The minute it sounded I was halfway to the door.

"Hey, Zack," Danny called out. "You want me to save a seat for you in the cafeteria?"

"Sure, Danny," I answered. I wasn't going to the cafeteria. But I didn't want anyone to know that I was leaving school in the middle of the day.

When I was sure no one was watching, I slipped through the front door and burst outside.

I raced down Hawthorne Street to Canyon Drive.

I ran so hard I thought my lungs would burst. But I didn't stop. There was no time.

I reached Marcy's house in under five minutes.

And as I neared her front gate, I knew something was wrong.

The front door banged open and shut in the wind.

I sprinted up the walk.

Yes. Something was definitely wrong.

The glass in the big front window—it was totally shattered!

16

A man walked out the front door. A stranger with a dark brown beard. He wore a tool belt around his waist.

"Who are you?" I blurted. "Where are the Novis?"

"I'm from the glass company," the man told me. "I'm here to fix the window."

"Where is everyone?"

"The whole family left this morning," the man answered. He measured the new glass. "Some kind of family emergency."

"What kind of emergency?" I demanded.

"An emergency is all my boss told me," the man said.

"Do you know who broke the window?" I asked.

"No," he said, shaking his head. "But it's too bad. A window this big is hard to replace."

"Do you think it could have been some kind of explosion?" I asked.

"Could have been, I suppose," the man replied. "But when I checked the gas line, there was no sign of a leak. Kind of funny, isn't it?"

It wasn't funny at all.

I knew who was responsible.

Miss Gaunt.

What did she do to Marcy's family?

Suddenly I felt sick.

I wanted to go home.

But I couldn't. I had to warn my friends in school. I had to tell them how dangerous Miss Gaunt was.

I barely made it back to Shadyside Middle before the bell rang. Miss Gaunt brought the class to order.

I waited for a good time to write a note to Chris. But Miss Gaunt was staring at me every time I looked up. She kept her eyes on me all through geography and math.

70

"We'll spend the last hour on spelling," Miss Gaunt announced.

"Miss Prescott always teaches social studies on Tuesday afternoon," Tiffany complained.

"What is it you like so much about social studies, dear?"

"We were studying crop rotation," Tiffany said. "I liked reading about farmers—and how they keep feeding the soil to make things grow better."

"A sweet girl like you interested in dirt?" Miss Gaunt asked. "Why not wait till you're older to study nasty things like that?"

"Does that mean no social studies?" Tiffany asked.

"Not as long as I'm in charge," Miss Gaunt replied. "But how would you like to spell *rotation* for us?"

Tiffany sighed and walked up to the blackboard.

I knew I couldn't wait any longer.

It was time to spread the word about Miss Gaunt.

I ripped a sheet of paper from my notebook.

"Miss Gaunt is a ghost," I wrote. "I have proof. Be very carefull." I folded the paper and wrote Chris's name on the outside.

The seat in front of me was empty—Marcy's

seat. So I slipped the note to Debbie Steinford to my right. She's the class goody-goody, but I didn't think she'd tell Miss Gaunt.

Debbie shot me a dirty look, but she grabbed the note anyway. I watched her read Chris's name.

As Miss Gaunt watched Tiffany finish writing *rotation* on the board, Debbie passed the note to Ezra Goldstein in the row ahead of her.

Ezra passed the note to Danny Abernathy ahead of him.

Chris sat in the first row. I held my breath as Danny passed the note to him.

My eyes were glued to Chris as he unfolded the note under his desk.

He pushed his chair back.

Then he bent over to steal a better glimpse. When that didn't work, he spread the note out flat on top of his desk.

I saw him shake his head.

Then he turned around in his chair and flashed me that big stupid grin of his!

I checked the front of the class. Miss Gaunt had called Bobby Dreyfuss up to the board. He was trying to spell *artichoke.*

"A-R-T-A," Bobby spelled aloud as he wrote.

I heard someone snicker. A familiar snicker. Chris, of course.

"Christopher?" Miss Gaunt asked, looming over him. "What's that on you're desk?"

"It's nothing, Miss Gaunt," Chris said. He shoved the note in his pocket.

Bang! Bang! Bang!

Miss Gaunt slammed her pointer on his desk.

"Christopher!" she demanded. "Give me that note!"

17

Don't let me down, Chris! I thought. Just this once, keep your big mouth shut!

Chris reached into his pocket.

Throw it out the window, I begged silently. Or use that big mouth of yours to chew it up and swallow it.

If Miss Gaunt lays her bony hands on it, I'm in major trouble.

Chris held out the note. "This note, Miss Gaunt?" he asked timidly.

Thanks, Chris, I thought. Thanks a lot.

She snatched the note from him and read it carefully.

What if she recognizes my handwriting?

What if she realizes I wrote the note?

My mouth turned dry. I tried to swallow, but I couldn't. My hands began to shake so I hid them under my desk.

"A ghost," Miss Gaunt announced slowly. "Someone has accused *me* of being a ghost!"

Miss Gaunt paced slowly up and down the aisles. Studying each kid in the class.

"Can you imagine why someone would say that about me, Tiffany?" she asked.

Tiffany opened her mouth, then shut it. She shook her head.

Even Tiffany couldn't speak. And she's never afraid to talk.

"Can you imagine such a thing, Ezra?"

Ezra shook his head, too. He stared down at his desk.

"Well, one of you imagined it," Miss Gaunt said, her little voice growing higher and louder. "Or you wouldn't have written such a thing in the first place!"

Miss Gaunt stopped at Debbie's desk. "Did you write the note, Debbie?" she asked.

"No, Miss Gaunt," Debbie mumbled.

"Can you imagine why someone would say that

I am a ghost?" Miss Gaunt asked. "Is it because I am not as young as I used to be?"

"I don't know, Miss Gaunt," Debbie said. "You don't look so old to me."

Yeah, right! I thought. Miss Gaunt is at least two hundred years old! Can't anyone else see that?

"Thank you, my dear." Miss Gaunt patted Debbie on the shoulder.

Debbie shivered.

Miss Gaunt proceeded down the next aisle.

She was closing in on me.

I checked the clock. Five minutes left to the end of class.

Miss Gaunt paused at Danny's desk.

"Is it because I wear white?" Miss Gaunt asked him. "Is *that* why I have been called a ghost?"

"Maybe," Danny said, shrugging.

"Do you think it's nice to call someone a ghost?" Miss Gaunt asked.

"I would *never* call anyone a ghost, Miss Gaunt," Danny said. "That's for sure."

"That's because you are a very sensitive person," she said as she glided across the room to the next aisle. "You would never be so unkind."

I glanced at the clock again.

Only three minutes left before the final bell.

Maybe she won't make it to me, I prayed.

"You can't imagine what it's like to be a substitute teacher," Miss Gaunt continued. "You hardly know a soul. You feel so alone. Then someone starts spreading unkind rumors." She spun around and glared at Bobby Dreyfuss. "How do you think that makes me feel?"

"Not good, I guess," Bobby answered, his lips quivering.

Miss Gaunt slammed her pointer down on his desk so hard he jumped out of his seat.

"Exactly!" Miss Gaunt screeched. "Let me tell you, boys and girls, gossip is not a pretty thing. Gossip is cruel. And what do we do to people who are cruel?"

Bobby stared up at her. "I-I guess we punish them," he stuttered.

"Punish them!" Miss Gaunt's voice grew even louder. "Very good, Bobby. That's exactly what we do. We punish them!"

I started to break out into a cold sweat. Tiny beads of perspiration dripped down my forehead.

If Miss Gaunt looks at me now, she'll know.

She'll know I wrote that note.

She'll know I said she was a ghost.

I checked the clock.

One minute left.

One minute until the bell.

"Don't worry, boys and girls," Miss Guant said, the tone of her voice suddenly soft and gentle. "I am not going to pursue this matter any further. I just want everyone to know that whoever wrote this note has hurt my feelings deeply. Very deeply."

The bell rang.

I could hardly believe my luck.

She didn't find out that I wrote the note!

I scooped up my backpack and raced to the door—and felt an icy hand squeeze my shoulder.

Miss Gaunt's hand.

"Zachariah," she said sweetly. "I am afraid I have to ask you to stay after class today!"

18

"**B**ut I-I've got to get home, Miss Gaunt," I stammered. "My mom's expecting me."

"This won't take but a moment, dear," she said.

A moment was way too long to be alone with a ghost.

But I didn't have any choice.

"Sorry," Chris mouthed on his way out the door.

Tiffany smiled sympathetically. But most of the other kids didn't even glance at me. They rushed out with their eyes glued to the floor.

When the last kid left, Miss Gaunt shut the

door. The quiet little click the lock made sent a chill down my spine.

Then she turned toward me. "You're frightened, aren't you, Zachariah?"

I nodded slowly.

"Lots of things scare you. Don't they, Zachariah?" she said. "That's why you bought that book *Power Kids,* isn't it?"

"N-no one knows about that," I stammered. "How could—"

"Oh, I noticed you in the bookstore," Miss Gaunt said. "It was the day before I started here. I visited town. To stretch my legs. And get the cobwebs out of my hair, so to speak. And I couldn't help thinking, 'What a fine boy. He'd be perfect.'"

Perfect for what? I wondered. *Perfect for what?*

"And here I was—just about to take over another class. But as soon as I spotted you, I knew I had to arrange for your teacher to come down with a cold. A nasty cold. It was naughty of me, I suppose, but I just couldn't resist!"

"Y-you made Miss Prescott sick?" I asked.

"I'm sorry to say I did. But I knew I *had* to be *your* teacher!"

Miss Gaunt approached her desk. She unfolded the note and read it again.

Maybe I can tell her the note was a joke, I thought. A stupid Halloween joke.

No. There's no way she'd believe me.

"What can I say, Zachariah?" Miss Gaunt asked. "Except that today I am very disappointed in you."

I was trapped!

And scared.

Really scared.

What was Miss Gaunt going to do to me?

She continued on. "You need to work on your spelling, dear." She held the note up in front of me. *"Careful* has only one *l.* Fortunately for you, your error won't influence your final grade."

Spelling! She wanted to talk to me about spelling?

"You're right, Miss Gaunt," I said quickly. "I'll go straight home and start studying."

"That won't be necessary, Zachariah."

Keep her talking, I told myself. Maybe Chris will wonder what's taking me so long. And he'll come back.

"Um. Is that how you knew I wrote the note?" I asked. "Because of the spelling?"

"Not entirely," Miss Gaunt said. "You followed me to the cemetery yesterday. You discovered the grave—and the truth. So you see—you were the only one who could have written that note."

"Marcy could have!" I blurted.

"Well, we don't have to worry about her anymore. Do we?"

"What did you do to her?" I croaked. I was so frightened now, I nearly choked on my own words. "Where—where is she?"

"You know, Zachariah, I do not understand why you had to drag her along. She could have ruined everything."

I glanced behind me. Could I jump through one of the windows? I wondered.

Miss Gaunt placed the note on her desk and reached into a drawer. She lifted out a silver-wrapped box, topped with a shiny black bow.

"Ah!" she cried. "Enough about Marcy. I have a present for you."

What would a ghost give as a present? I didn't want to find out.

"That's okay, Miss Gaunt. You don't have to give me anything."

Could I push past her and escape?

"Nonsense, Zachariah," Miss Gaunt replied. "I want to give you a present. After all, *you* are my favorite student."

"What about Debbie Steinford?" The words

82

flew out of my mouth. "All the teachers love Debbie!"

"No. No. Zachariah. This is for you. To open later."

She shoved the package into my backpack. I didn't know what was in it—and I didn't want to know.

Miss Gaunt scooped up the note from her desk. She tore it up and threw the shreds in the waste-basket.

"No one believed your silly note," she said. "Which is certainly a nice piece of luck for me. I suspect the principal wouldn't be very happy if he knew I was a ghost!"

"I promise I won't tell anyone. You're a wonder-ful teacher, Miss Gaunt. I won't do anything to get you in trouble!"

Miss Gaunt smiled at me. "Do you really think I am a wonderful teacher, Zachariah?"

"Definitely. I've learned tons from you," I told her.

"Yes. You are correct. I am a wonderful teacher. And it's just not fair," Miss Gaunt said. "Can you imagine that I can leave my grave only once every ten years—the week before Halloween? That's not very often, is it?"

83

"No, Miss Gaunt," I agreed. "That's not very often."

How was I going to escape? I had to find a way out!

"And what's worse," she continued, "is that on the stroke of twelve on Halloween night I must return to my grave. Which is why I try to make the most of my time. I love every second of it, too. But especially the Halloween party. Do you like Halloween parties, Zachariah?"

"Oh, sure, Miss Gaunt," I answered nervously. "Who doesn't like Halloween parties?"

If I ran for it, would she try to catch me?

"Do you know what the highlight of the party is for me?" she asked.

I shook my head.

"The highlight is when I pick my favorite student," she said.

"What do you pick a student for?" My voice cracked.

"You know, don't you?" Miss Gaunt said. "That's why you're so frightened, isn't it?"

"I don't know anything. I don't know what you want with me. I don't want to know, Miss Gaunt. Please, let me go home," I begged.

She's never going to let me leave!

"Allow me to explain," Miss Gaunt began.

84

"Every ten years I select one student to take back with me," she said.

"Back with you?" I gasped. "Back where?"

"Why, back to the grave, of course," she said. "Back to the grave—to become a ghost like me. And then I will be able to teach them—forever!"

"I don't want to go with you, Miss Gaunt! I want to stay here in Shadyside!"

"But I need you, Zachariah," she said. "You're so much brighter than the others."

"I am not brighter," I protested. "I'm not good at decimals. I'm not good at spelling. You just said so yourself!"

"Ah, but you guessed what other children couldn't even imagine about me."

"No!" I shouted. "I won't go!"

"Oh, Zachariah." Miss Gaunt pouted. "Aren't you even a tiny bit pleased?"

I didn't trust myself to speak. I was afraid if I opened my mouth I would start screaming. And never stop.

I ran to the door.

I twisted the lock.

As I swung the door open, Miss Gaunt called after me. "Halloween . . . tomorrow, Zachariah. Midnight! To join our dark, dark world—of ghosts."

19

Her grave!

She's planning to take me back to her grave!

And make me a ghost!

I ran from the classroom.

I pounded down the hall. I slammed through the school's big double doors. And jumped off the top step, flying to the ground. Then I raced down Hawthorne as fast as I could.

The white strips of cloth hanging from the oak tree on the corner whipped across my face. I didn't slow down.

Jack-o'-lanterns leered at my from every porch.

Jack-o'-lanterns for Halloween.

I slipped on some wet leaves and nearly fell.

Don't stop, I told myself. Just get home. Get home and don't come out until Halloween is over.

I ran so hard I thought my chest would explode.

Home, I thought every time one of my feet hit the cement.

Home, home, home, home.

I turned a corner. I was nearly there!

I dashed past the neighbors' houses. Then I cut across my lawn and charged up to the door.

It was locked.

I shoved my hands into my pockets. Empty. What did I do with my key?

I hammered on the door. "Let me in!" I screamed.

What if Miss Gaunt realizes I'm never coming out of the house? What if she's on her way here? What if she decides to take me back to her grave—now?

I beat on the door with both fists.

"Who is it?" I heard my brother, Kevin, call in a high voice.

"Kevin, let me in!" I hollered.

"We don't need anything. Have a nice day!" Kevin trilled.

"Kevin, open it! Now! Or I'm calling Mom!"

"Mom's not home!" Kevin yelled back.

I rammed my shoulder against the door the way they do in cop shows. I didn't care if I broke the door down. I had to get inside.

I threw myself at the door again. And as I did, Kevin opened it. I soared into the hallway.

Kevin laughed like an idiot.

I slammed the door and locked it. I slid the chain in place.

Kevin leaned against the wall. Watching. "I knew Halloween would drive you completely insane some year," he told me.

I ignored him. I ran around to the back door and locked it. Then I made sure every window was locked.

Are ghosts like vampires? I wondered. Do they have to be invited in before they can enter a house?

I hurried upstairs and checked all the windows up there, too. I triple-checked my own window. Then I threw myself facedown on my bed.

My backpack opened and something slid out.

Miss Gaunt's present.

I threw it on the floor.

And stared at it.

Miss Gaunt had wrapped it carefully. The corners were nice and smooth. The black bow was arranged just so.

What is in it? I wondered. Some gross dead thing? Or something worse? Something alive? Is it safe to have it in the house?

I sat up and nudged the present with my toe. I didn't hear anything. I gave the package a kick. Nothing.

I knelt down and ran my fingers over the silver paper. It felt like a book.

I slowly tore away a corner of the paper. I was right. A book.

I inhaled deeply.

A book.

That's not so bad.

I ripped the rest of the paper away.

My stomach lurched when I read the front cover.

The title said: *The Book of the Dead.*

20

*T*he Book of the Dead.

I touched the cover with the tip of one finger. I expected it to feel cold—like Miss Gaunt.

But it didn't. It felt warm.

I opened it up—and spotted my name! I slammed the book shut.

I'm throwing this thing out, I decided. There's nothing in *The Book of the Dead* that I need to know. At least not for a long, *long* time.

I grabbed the book and tossed it in the waste-basket.

Wait, I thought. Maybe I should read the part that has my name in it.

I flipped open the cover. It was an inscription and it said:

> For Zachariah,
> Welcome!
> Your teacher *forever,*
> Evangeline Gaunt.

No way, I thought. No way!

I noticed again how warm the book felt. It started to pulse under my fingertips. As if it were alive.

I flung it back into the trash.

Don't flip out, I told myself. Don't flip out. You just have to make it through one more day. At midnight on Halloween this will all be over.

I headed back downstairs. Usually I avoid Kevin—especially when Mom and Dad aren't around to referee. But I was terrified, and I didn't want to be by myself.

Chris called on the phone about a million times, but I made Kevin tell him I wasn't feeling well.

After dinner I hung around my parents. It would be pretty hard for Miss Gaunt to drag me away from them, I figured. I could tell my parents thought I was acting weird, but they didn't say anything about it.

After my favorite TV show ended, Mom said it was time for bed.

Sleep. Upstairs. Alone.

"Can't I stay up a little bit longer?" I begged.

"Sorry, Zach," she replied. "You know it's a school night."

I practically crawled up the stairs. But when I reached my room, I sprinted inside and jumped between the sheets of my bed. Then I tugged the covers up to my chin.

Every time I closed my eyes, I imagined myself lying in a grave. With thousands of swollen worms wriggling underneath me.

So I stayed up all night.

Trying to come up with a plan.

A plan to stay home from school.

My life depended on it!

The next morning I leaped out of bed.

I slipped into the bathroom and closed the door. I turned on the hot water in the bathtub and let it run. I wanted the bathroom to be nice and steamy.

After about five minutes my pajamas began to stick to me. Now I appeared all sweaty.

I drenched a washcloth in hot tap water, and I wrung it out. Then I pressed it to my forehead. Instant fever!

92

I bolted downstairs before my fake fever cooled.

"You'd better get dressed, honey," Mom said as I entered the kitchen. "You don't want to be late for school."

Yes, I do, I thought. I want to be so late that I won't arrive there till tomorrow.

She held out a glass of orange juice. I pushed it away. I sagged into my chair. "I don't feel so well," I moaned.

Kevin wandered in and plopped down across the table. He snagged my juice.

Mom placed her hand on my forehead. "You do feel a little warm," she commented.

"Check his pulse," Kevin said. "Just to see if he has one."

"Be nice," Mom said. "Your poor brother isn't feeling well. You go back to bed, honey. I'll bring you something to eat in a few minutes."

Before Mom started talking about calling the doctor, I darted upstairs. I turned on the TV and tuned into some lame game shows.

But I watched the clock more than I watched the television—counting down the time until I was safe from Miss Gaunt.

At four o'clock I couldn't decide whether I should be relieved—or more scared than ever. The

Halloween party was over. But it was hours until midnight.

And now that school was out, Miss Gaunt could be anywhere. I had eight more hours to go. Eight long hours.

The next two hours I didn't even pretend to watch TV. I stared at the clock. Gazing at the seconds and minutes ticking away.

Mom popped into my room at six o'clock. She felt my forehead. "Good!" she exclaimed. No more fever! Are you ready for Halloween?" she asked.

I nearly gasped. "I-uh-thought I wasn't allowed out today."

"Wouldn't you like to greet the trick-or-treaters at the door?"

"Oh, sure," I answered. Boy, was I relieved.

"Great costume, Zack," Kevin called as I came down the stairs.

"I'm not wearing a costume," I snapped.

"Sure you are. You're the Big Pain!" Kevin laughed. "You'll do anything to get out of Halloween, won't you?" he demanded. "You can fool Mom, but you can't fool me."

I ignored him. He shuffled off to the kitchen.

The doorbell rang.

I grabbed the bowl of candy Mom had set out on the hall table.

I pulled open the door.

"Trick or treat! Trick or treat!"

A bunch of little kids perched on the porch. I could see their mothers waiting for them on the sidewalk. I dropped candy in each of their bags.

The doorbell rang again.

"Trick or treat! Trick or treat!"

A Martian, a dinosaur, and a ballerina appeared.

I handed out the candy—and even pretended to be frightened of the tiny dinosaur. The kids giggled as I closed the door.

The doorbell rang again.

It's going to be a busy night, I thought. Halloween will be over before I know it!

I opened the door.

Only one person stood there.

"Trick or treat, Zachariah!"

Miss Gaunt!

21

I froze in the doorway. I stared at the white gauzy gown. The white gloves. The veil.

It was Miss Gaunt! She had come for me!

"You can't come in!" I shouted. "I won't let you."

"Zack, honey?" Mom ran in from the kitchen. "Is everything okay?"

I clutched Mom's arm. "It's Miss Gaunt. My substitute teacher!" I cried. "Don't let her take me away!"

"Let me feel your forehead," Mom said. "Maybe you do have a fever."

"She wants to kidnap me!" I screamed as Mom lifted her hand to my forehead. "She is going to kill me and make me live in the graveyard!"

"But, Zack—" Mom started.

"Save me, Mom," I interrupted. "You've got to save me!"

"But, Zack," Mom said again. "Miss Gaunt isn't here. It's just . . ."

Then I heard the laughter. I turned. Miss Gaunt had lifted her veil. And underneath—it wasn't Miss Gaunt at all.

It was Chris. And now he was doubled over, laughing his head off.

"Did I really look like her?" Chris asked between gasps of laughter.

"You know you look *exactly* like her!" I said. "You did this on purpose. Just to scare me!"

"I thought it would be funny," Chris said, still chuckling. "Besides, I didn't come over just to scare you. I came to see how you were feeling."

"Why, isn't that nice of him?" Mom said. "Would you like a treat, Chris?"

"Thanks, Mrs. Pepper," Chris said. He strolled over to the treat table. Once Mom headed back to the kitchen, he started cramming candy bars into his pillowcase.

"Anyone notice I was sick?" I asked Chris. "Besides you, I mean?"

"Miss Gaunt noticed. And boy, did she seem upset. She really *is* nuts about you."

"Upset how?" I asked. "Was she, um, sad-upset—or angry-upset?"

"More like brokenhearted-upset," Chris said. "I have to admit, it was a little weird."

Chris shook his pillowcase to make room for more candy. Then he continued. "Anyway, Miss Gaunt told us that Miss Prescott will be back on Monday. Miss Gaunt said she was really sorry to leave without saying goodbye to you and Marcy."

"Has anybody heard from Marcy?" I asked anxiously.

"Nah. But I passed her house coming here. The window is fixed. I'm sure she'll be home soon."

That's what you think, I muttered under my breath.

"What?" Chris asked. His pillowcase was full now, and he was getting ready to leave.

I knew Chris would never believe me. But I had to try to convince him. "Miss Gaunt is a ghost!" I shouted. "And she's done something horrible to Marcy and her family."

98

"Oh, right," Chris said sarcastically. "I read your stupid note."

"She really is a ghost. And she got rid of Marcy because we saw her grave."

"What grave?"

"Her grave. Miss Gaunt's grave! It said 'Born 1769. Died 1845.'"

"You saw *her* grave?" Chris asked. "With her name on it?"

"Yes!" I answered with a sigh of relief. It looked as if Chris was finally beginning to believe me.

Chris set his pillowcase on the floor. "Hmmm. I know. It was probably her great-great-great grandmother's grave."

"But the grave was empty!" I cried.

"That doesn't prove she's a ghost, Zack."

"Look, Chris. Marcy's gone. Gone because we saw Miss Gaunt's grave. Because we know the truth. Miss Gaunt is a ghost. Why won't you believe me? She told me that she wants to take me back with her to the graveyard. Tonight. Why would she say that if she weren't a ghost?"

"For special math tutoring?" Chris asked, starting to laugh again.

"No! NO! NO!" I screamed. "She wants to turn me into a ghost, too."

99

"Well, maybe you won't be afraid of ghosts anymore—once you're one of them." Chris laughed so hard now he had to clutch his sides.

"What's all the laughing about?" Mom asked, coming up beside me. "Are you feeling better?"

"No, Mom. I'm not feeling better. In fact, I feel a lot worse," I said, glaring at Chris.

"Well, why don't you go up to bed?" Mom replied. "Get some rest. I have to go next door for a few minutes. Come on, Chris. I'll walk you out."

Chris and Mom left. I practically slammed the door behind them. I noticed Chris's pillowcase on the floor. He had left it behind. Well, too bad. He wasn't getting it back.

I started up the stairs to bed when the doorbell rang again. "Kevin!" I yelled for my brother. "Get the door!"

No answer.

Great. I muttered. Kevin never does anything around here. I'll be answering the door all night.

The doorbell rang again.

"Okay. Okay. I'm coming."

As I approached the door, I could hear the shouts of the trick-or-treaters outside. I wished Halloween were over.

I yanked the door open. It was Chris.

"Forget it! I'm not giving you your stupid candy!" I shouted.

"Candy? I didn't come for candy, Zachariah. I came for you!"

It was Miss Gaunt.

The real Miss Gaunt!

22

Miss Gaunt reached out a gloved hand and grasped me tightly by the wrist.

"No!" I shrieked. "I won't go! I don't want to be a ghost!"

"It doesn't matter what you want!" she said calmly. "Don't you understand that?"

She didn't sound like an old lady anymore. Her voice was strong—and mean. And her grip was like iron.

She yanked me forward, dragging me toward the front door. I grabbed the doorknob to the front closet. I tried to pull myself back.

"Help!" I screamed. "Help!"

I heard footsteps coming down the stairs. Kevin.

As soon as he appeared, Miss Gaunt loosened her grip. "Hello, there," Miss Gaunt said. "I'm Zachariah's substitute teacher. I stopped by to invite him to a Halloween party."

"Don't believe her!" I cried. "Our class Halloween party was this afternoon!"

Kevin studied Miss Gaunt. "Hey, that's a really cool costume," he finally said. Then he turned to me. "Zack, you're pathetic. You'd say anything to skip Halloween."

"Actually, Zack is right. Our class Halloween party was this afternoon," Miss Gaunt said sweetly. "But some of the children thought it would be nice to have another one tonight. It would be a shame for Zack to miss that one, too."

"Don't let her take me!" I shrieked. "She's going to force me into the graveyard and turn me into a ghost—just like her!"

"Are you really going to turn Zack into a ghost?" Kevin laughed.

"I promised him I would," Miss Gaunt said. "I think it's important for grown-ups to live up to their promises. Don't you?"

"Well, have a great time at the party," Kevin said, heading up the stairs.

I tried to run after him, but Miss Gaunt was way too fast for me. She lunged for my arm. Her grip felt strong enough to crush my bones.

She jerked me down our front path onto the sidewalk. As we passed our neighbor's house, I screamed. "Mom! Come out! Mom!" But she couldn't hear me.

My shoes scraped the sidewalk as Miss Gaunt yanked on my arm. I thought she was going to pull it right out of its socket.

My eyes searched the street for help. Two kids dressed as aliens were approaching us.

"Help! Help!" I screamed.

"Oooh! Oooh!" they giggled.

"She's going to turn me into a ghost!" I cried.

"Really?" one of the aliens asked.

"I'm certainly going to do my best," Miss Gaunt replied in her thin, breathy voice.

The kids laughed and jogged up the steps to the next house.

Miss Gaunt gripped my arm tighter. Practically lifting me off the ground. We glided down the street.

"Help me!" I begged two masked bandits. "She's kidnapping me!"

But the bandits laughed, too.

We turned down Fear Street.

104

There were no trick-or-treaters. No one out. The street was deserted. The air—perfectly still. Nothing moved.

A dim light shone through the window of a house every now and then. But mostly it was dark. And creepy. As creepy as the night Marcy and I followed Miss Gaunt on our bikes.

"Miss Gaunt, please don't do this. Please," I begged, struggling to free myself.

"But I have to, Zachariah," Miss Gaunt answered. "You're such a good student. I want to teach you—forever."

I tried to rip my arm from Miss Gaunt's grasp. She clamped down harder. Nothing could stop her. She glided faster down Fear Street, dragging me behind.

We reached a corner. And turned.

We had come to the Fear Street Cemetery.

"Home, Zachariah," Miss Gaunt announced. "Home at last!"

23

~~~~~

"**N**o way!" I screamed. "I'm not going in there. You're never going to get away with this!"

"But I already have!" she cackled.

I twisted in Miss Gaunt's grip. But she had the strength of a wrestler.

I opened my mouth wide and sank my teeth into the folds of her gauzy sleeve. I heard a sickening crunch. Her arm snapped. I had broken her bone. In the moonlight I glimpsed the jagged edge poking through her sleeve. But it didn't seem to matter. Her grip was as strong as ever.

"Don't do that again," Miss Gaunt warned.

"You don't want to make me cross, do you, Zachariah?"

We entered the Fear Street Cemetery. And I spotted a familiar-looking man. It was Mr. Sangfwad from Shop Till You Drop (Dead!).

What was he doing in the cemetery? Could he save me?

"Mr. Sangfwad!" I yelled. "Help me! Mr. Sangfwad!"

Mr. Sangfwad turned toward me. But he made no effort to help. He didn't seem to recognize me.

"It's me!" I screamed. "Zack Pepper. I was in your store the other day."

"Ah," he said as he moved closer. And then I realized why Mr. Sangfwad didn't know who I was. His eyes were gone! Two empty sockets stared out into the darkness.

Mr. Sangfwad was a ghost, too!

"Welcome to our little party," he said. Then he wiped some drool from his bony chin.

"Let me go," I begged. "I want to go home."

"But the party's just begun," Miss Gaunt crooned.

"I don't want to be at this party!" I cried out. "I don't belong here."

"But you're the life of the party!" Mr. Sangfwad cackled. "At least until midnight."

"Wh-what happens at midnight?" I asked.

Mr. Sangfwad placed his face close to mine. I tried to shrink back from his foul breath. But Miss Gaunt held me firmly.

His lips brushed my ear as he whispered into it. "At midnight you will become the un-life of the party. You will turn into a ghost—just like us."

Then Mr. Sangfwad threw back his head and shrieked—like a madman.

"I don't want to be a ghost!" I cried over his awful howls.

"I am afraid Zachariah isn't in a party mood tonight," Miss Gaunt said. "It was nice to see you, Mr. Sangfwad. But we must be on our way."

Miss Gaunt tugged me deeper into the grave-yard. But we could still hear Mr. Sangfwad's shrieks echoing all around us.

The air grew colder as we plunged deeper still. The graves in this part of the cemetery were older and smaller. I tried to focus on them, but we were moving too fast. They passed in a blur.

And then, finally, we stopped.

At a grave.

The open grave Marcy and I had seen before.

Only this time, a coffin rested within it.

And the lid was open. Waiting.

Waiting for us.

24

"**Y**ou can't make me go down there," I screeched. "I won't let you!"

"Oh, Zachariah," Miss Gaunt said. "It's no use fighting. Can't you see that?"

"But I don't want to go with you!" I pleaded. "I want to go home."

"But this *is* your home," Miss Gaunt said. "Come, Zachariah. It is time."

"No!" I screamed. "I won't! I can't!"

I pushed back with all my strength. The force set me free! My head hit the ground with a thud. Right next to the open grave.

I gazed up. Miss Gaunt was calmly peeling off one of her white gloves.

I inched my way back. Back. Sliding along the wet grass.

Miss Gaunt moved forward. Slowly. Then her arm shot out. And before I could dodge away, her bare bony fingers were digging deep into my shoulder.

She lifted me up with one hand. "Come with me, Zachariah," she whispered.

My strength faded. My legs began to tremble. Step by step, my feet slipped across the grass as Miss Gaunt pulled me forward.

I hovered at the edge of the grave now. Peering down. Down at the open coffin.

Miss Gaunt stood beside me. "Welcome home, Zachariah," she said, with a soft cackle. And then she shoved me. One quick hard shove.

And before I knew it, I was falling.

Falling into Miss Gaunt's grave.

Into the open coffin.

25

⟡

"**H**elp!" I screamed. "Help!"

I landed facedown in the coffin.

"Comfy, isn't it?" Miss Gaunt purred from above.

I scrambled to my feet. I threw myself against the side of the grave, struggling to climb out. I clutched at the dirt—trying to pull myself up. But the ancient soil crumbled beneath my grip.

"Help!" I screamed again. "Someone, help me!"

"My goodness, Zachariah," Miss Gaunt said. "Please. Not so loud. You're going to wake up the dead." And then she laughed. Not her wispy laugh—a deep, cruel laugh.

I reached up. Groping at the wall of the grave. My fingers wrapped around a thick tree root. I dug my hands into the dirt and grasped the root tightly. I began to hoist myself out.

"Save your strength," Miss Gaunt called down. "You can't escape. It's much too late for that. It's almost midnight."

"No!" I cried out. "I'm not staying here with you!"

"I'm afraid you have no choice, dear," she said, kneeling beside the grave, peering down. "Just think how lovely it's going to be. Think of all the time we'll have together. All the things I'll be able to teach you. After all, I am a wonderful teacher."

I reached up—to shove Miss Gaunt back. But my hand caught her veil—ripping it away.

"What have you done?" Miss Gaunt shrieked. She jerked up and turned to search the ground for her veil.

I clutched the tree root tightly. I jammed one foot into the dirt. Then I pushed up with the other foot with all my strength.

I sprang up.

I held on to the tree root with one hand and reached out for the grave's opening with the other. Then I pulled myself out.

I jumped quickly to my feet.

Miss Gaunt whirled around.

And her face was gone!

No flesh.

Just a bony skull holding a few wisps of gray hair. And worms. Slimy purple worms. Crawling in and out of the sockets where her eyes should have been.

I choked back a scream. My hands flew to my eyes, covering them.

"Look at me, Zachariah," Miss Gaunt ordered.

"I can't!" I shrieked, gasping for breath.

"You must," she commanded harshly. Then her voice softened. "You must, Zachariah. You must. Because in a few minutes, you will look exactly like this, too."

My hands floated away from my eyes. Moving by themselves—controlled by Miss Gaunt. I stared into her horrifying face.

"You can't get away from me!" she said. "I'm never going to let you go. Never!"

I glanced down at her hands. Her raw, bony fingers twitched in the moonlight.

Then they shot out and curled around my neck.

"Let me go!" I shrieked. I tried to pry her fingers from my throat, but she was too strong.

I struggled hard. She shoved me back. My foot

114

dangled over the open grave. I was losing my balance.

In the distance the town clock began to strike midnight. One . . . Two . . . Three . . .

Footsteps. It was difficult to tell, but I thought I heard footsteps.

Miss Gaunt heard them, too.

She snapped her head up. She peered over my shoulder. Her body stiffened.

She lifted a bony finger and pointed. "Wh-who is . . ."

What could possibly scare *her* this much?

I whirled around.

It was another Miss Gaunt!

26

~~~~

Another Miss Gaunt—with big white high-tops peeking out from under her white dress. Chris!

I was never so glad to see him in my life!

"Come on! Help me!" I cried out. I grabbed Miss Gaunt's spindly arm and swung her into the coffin.

Then I slammed the lid down and jumped on top of the coffin. It rumbled underneath me.

"Come on, Chris! Help me hold this thing down, now!"

The clock continued to chime. Seven . . . Eight . . .

Chris jumped down next to me. His "Miss

Gaunt" veil flew up in his face as the wind began to blow. Then the whole ground shook.

The coffin lid jerked open and a howling wind escaped from inside the casket!

We slammed the lid down again. It snapped open once more—with a force that sent dirt flinging from the grave.

"Hold it down!" I screamed. "Hold it down!"

Nine . . .

The wind howled in our ears. Soil and rocks whipped around us. Pelting us.

There were only seconds left until midnight. Seconds before Miss Gaunt returned to the world of ghosts. Seconds before I was safe—finally.

Ten . . .

The coffin lid wrenched open and a bony hand shot out! It grabbed me by the ankle.

"Oh, no! Not now!" I shrieked. I kicked wildly to free myself—before it was too late. But the harder I struggled, the tighter her grip grew.

Eleven . . .

I was slipping—slipping into the coffin. Slipping away—forever.

Twelve!

A jagged bolt of lightning sliced through the sky. It pierced the ground next to the grave.

Miss Gaunt's bony hand suddenly dropped

from my leg. I watched in horror as it shriveled up and shrank back into the coffin.

Then the wind died. And the dirt storm settled.

The cemetery grew silent.

It was midnight. Halloween had ended.

I didn't realize I had been holding my breath. I let out a long sigh.

Chris and I pulled ourselves out of the grave.

"Thanks," I said, turning toward him. The color had completely drained from his face. Even his freckles were pale.

"I-I was walking by the cemetery," he stammered. "I heard someone screaming for help. It sounded like you."

"You showed up just in time!" I cried.

"I-I can't believe it," he said. "Miss Gaunt really was a ghost!"

Even in the moonlight, there was no mistaking the look on Chris's face. The look of horror. For the first time all week, I smiled.

27

"I decided to let you sleep in," Mom said when I walked into the kitchen Saturday morning. "I was afraid you didn't get enough sleep last night."

"I feel terrific, Mom," I said, chugging my juice.

"Well, I don't approve of your teacher keeping you out that late," Mom said. "And I'm going to talk to her about it."

"I don't think you can," I said. "Yesterday was her last day."

"I'll find her number in the telephone book," Mom replied. "What is her last name? Gaunt. Right?"

"Uh-huh," I said. "But I have a feeling her number is unlisted."

I grabbed a piece of toast and headed for the door. "See you later."

I raced over to Marcy's house. The window was fixed, but the house appeared deserted. I knocked on the door.

It slowly creaked open. And there she was!

"Marcy!" I cried. "You're here!"

Marcy stepped outside. She closed the door behind her very carefully. "Dad said not to slam the door," Marcy explained. "That's how he broke the window the other day."

Well, that explains one thing, I thought.

"Marcy, where *were* you?" I asked.

We sat on her front lawn. "It was the weirdest thing," she began. "After you rode off Thursday, I ran into the house. And Mom was on the phone. When she hung up she said we had to leave for my grandmother's house upstate right away."

"Did she say why?" I asked.

"Yes. She said Grandma was very sick."

"What's weird about that?" I asked.

"Wait," Marcy said, holding up her hand. Then she continued. "We jumped in the car. Dad drove all night. We reached Grandma's house Friday

120

morning. Grandma ran out of the house to meet us. And she was fine!"

"Pretty fast recovery, huh?" I said.

"No, Zack. *That* was the weird part. Grandma said she never called. She didn't know what Mom was talking about."

"I bet Miss Gaunt did it!" I cried. Then I told Marcy all about Halloween.

Marcy couldn't believe what had happened. "Well, at least no one will ever tease you about ghosts again."

"Yeah," I agreed. Then I jumped up. "Hey, there's Chris!" I waved him over.

"Chris, I was just telling Marcy all about Halloween."

"What about it?" Chris said.

Chris was playing it cool. I guess he couldn't bear the thought that I was right for once.

"Oh, just about Miss Gaunt being a ghost and all."

"Miss Gaunt? A ghost? Are you starting that again?"

"What do you mean?" I shouted in Chris's face. "Of course Miss Gaunt was a ghost. You saw her. You were in the cemetery with me! You were scared to death!"

Chris laughed. "Me? Scared? No way. That ghost stuff is strictly in *your* dreams, Zack. Not mine."

Chris didn't remember a thing. It was the last of Miss Gaunt's ghostly magic.

On Monday morning I walked to school by myself. When the school came into view, I reached into my backpack and pulled out Chris's snake. It was hard to believe—only a couple of weeks ago this thing terrified me.

I held the snake to my face and felt its slimy texture on my skin.

"Oshee ma terr hoom," I chanted softly. "Kubal den skaya!" It was one of the chants I had memorized from the book I rescued from the garbage—*The Book of the Dead.*

The rubber snake came to life. It slithered through my fingers. I patted it gently.

"So, Chris isn't scared of anything," I said to myself. "We'll see."

I ran up the stairs to Shadyside Middle School and raced down the hall. I learned a lot from Miss Gaunt, I thought as the snake slithered happily down into my backpack. Miss Gaunt was a wonderful teacher.

Are you ready for another walk
down Fear Street?
Turn the page for a terrifying
sneak preview.

THE ATTACK OF THE AQUA APES

Coming in mid-October 1995

The moment Scott came to the end of Park Drive, his heart started to beat a little faster. With just one step, he would cross the imaginary safety line into dangerous territory—Fear Street.

Even in the middle of the day, Fear Street seemed dark and scary. Enormous old trees lined both sides of the street. And as the sunlight tried to sneak through some of the huge branches, it cast strange shadows on the ground below. Shadows that looked like they could swallow you up.

Once you've walked down Fear Street, Scott

thought, you knew all the creepy stories you've heard about it were true.

"The adventure is about to begin!" Scott announced to Glen. He took a deep breath and started toward the Fear Street Woods. They were creepier than Fear Street. Scarier too.

The trees in the woods grew thick and gnarled—with black twisted branches that seemed to reach out. Reach out to strangle you.

Glen hesitated.

"Well, are you coming, or what?"

"This is a really stupid idea," Glen replied. "Why can't we follow the directions and use distilled water to grow the aqua apes."

"You're just chicken," Scott taunted. Then he started flapping his arms and squawking at Glen. *"Bawk, bawk, bawk!"*

"I am not chicken," Glen insisted.

"Then come on."

"There." Glen stepped into the woods. "Are you happy now?"

"This way," Scott pointed to the path ahead. The path that led directly to Fear Lake. "We'd better hurry. These woods get real dark, real early."

As they followed the trail, Scott noticed how quiet the woods were. He couldn't hear any birds chirping or crickets humming. Or any sound of life at all. Creepy. Really creepy.

Scott kept his eyes glued to the trail. He had to make sure that they stayed on the right path. No way was he getting lost in the Fear Street Woods.

"Can we hurry it up?" Glen asked. He followed Scott so closely that he stepped on the back of one of his sneakers.

"Do you have to walk on top of me?" Scott complained, yanking his sneaker back up. "The lake's right through there," he added, pointing straight ahead. "Relax."

"I'm telling you, this is a big mistake," Glen muttered as they reached the muddy banks of the lake.

"Just give me the tank," Scott ordered.

Glen pulled the little plastic tank out of his backpack and shoved it into Scott's hands.

Scott pulled off the top and handed it to Glen. Then he stepped up to the edge of the lake and dipped the open tank into the icy cold, blue water.

Other than being really, really cold, Scott didn't notice anything weird about the Fear Lake water. It wasn't gross, or smelly, or anything. In fact, it was clear. And Scott couldn't help feeling a little bit disappointed.

Scott held the tank out in front of him. "Okay,

now pour in the magic crystals," he instructed Glen.

"I don't see why we can't do this part back at your house," Glen complained. "It's starting to get dark."

"Bawk, bawk, bawk," Scott replied.

Glen fumbled around his backpack for the little packet of crystals. When he found it, he carefully tore the corner open.

"What do they look like?" Scott asked.

"Like sugar grains," Glen answered. He held the packet under Scott's nose for him to see.

"Pour them in," Scott ordered. He held the tank steady.

"Here goes nothing," Glen said. He shook the magic crystals into the tank.

The moment the first crystal hit the water from Fear Lake, Scott felt the tips of his fingers start to tingle.

Then the tiny tingling turned into a surge of electricity. It raced up his arms and snaked through his entire body.

He began to shake. Slightly, at first. Then wildly.

He tried to loosen his grip on the tank. But his fingers were stuck.

The tank began to crackle with electricity. Scott could see tiny lightning bolts shooting through the water. The water bubbled and churned.

Scott's heart pounded so hard and so fast, he was terrified that it would explode.

He opened his mouth to scream.

To scream for Glen to help him.

But no sound came out.

"Glen!" The name finally burst free from Scott's throat. "Help me!"

But the moment Scott screamed, the shock stopped.

His arms and legs grew still.

The water in the tank settled quietly.

"What's wrong?" Glen asked. "What happened?"

"I'm not exactly sure," Scott tried to explain. "When you poured in the crystals, a horrible shock raced through my whole body. It was the worst thing I've ever felt."

"Let's put the top on the tank and get out of here!" Glen cried.

Glen shoved the top on. Then he turned and charged toward the clearing.

"Wait for me!" Scott screamed, dashing after him.

They ran from the lake through the woods. And they didn't stop until they made it back to Scott's house and up the stairs to his room.

Scott carefully placed the tank in the center of his desk.

Then they both sat down on Scott's bed. Panting.

When they finally caught their breath, Scott bent down to peer into the water. "Oh, wow!" he shouted. "They're alive! It worked! We created aqua apes!"

Scott studied the aqua apes in the water. They were just little white specks. No bigger than dust specks in a beam of sunlight. But they *were* alive.

At first, they appeared to be floating aimlessly. But when Scott squinted for a better view, he could see that they were actually wiggling. Wiggling in different directions.

The aqua apes didn't look anything like the picture in the ad—or even in the picture on the box. But they were alive. And maybe they would grow into something cool.

"I don't see anything," Glen complained.

Glen was sitting on the middle of his bed. "You have to get closer," Scott told him. "They're real small."

Glen didn't budge.

"You're not going to get a shock," Scott told him. "I carried the tank all the way back here and nothing happened."

Glen stood up and crossed over to the tank. "I still can't see them," Glen insisted. "Where's your magnifying glass?"

Scott pulled a magnifying glass out of the top drawer of his desk and handed it to Glen.

"Pretty cool, huh?" Scott asked, as Glen studied the little creatures.

"Yeah," Glen agreed. "They are pretty cool. But wh—"

Glen's voice trailed off as he watched little air bubbles suddenly start floating up from the bottom of the tank.

"What's going on?" Scott asked. He grabbed the magnifying glass from Glen and peered into the bottom of the tank. The bubbles were shooting up from a crystal. A large black crystal.

"What is that?" Glen asked.

"I don't know," Scott answered.

The black crystal continued to fizz.

Scott and Glen watched it for a long time, waiting. Waiting for something more to happen.

But nothing did.

The black crystal simply continued to fizz.

The black crystal was still fizzing when Scott went to bed that night. He left the light on in the tank so he could watch it as he dozed off.

But the aqua apes were way too small for him to see from his bed. He couldn't even make out the black crystal from that far away. But he could see the air bubbles rising from it. Scott began counting the bubbles as they rose to the surface.

The numbers raced through his head faster and faster. His vision blurred as he focused on the bubbles.

Then the light in the tank went out. Scott figured the bulb in the tank lid blew. He'd check it out in the morning.

Scott pulled the covers up to his neck. As he rolled over to go to sleep, the light in the tank flashed on. And this time it glowed much brighter than before.

Scott turned toward it. I should just get up and turn it off, he thought. But before he could even throw back the covers, the light blinked off by itself again.

Then on.

Then off.

It continued to blink on and off until Scott slid out of bed. The moment his feet hit the floor, the light in the tank flared on and stayed on.

He walked toward the desk slowly. Cautiously. As he stepped closer, he noticed that the black crystal at the bottom of the tank was bubbling furiously. The water began churning. It turned from clear to murky. Then dark.

Scott reached out to turn off the light in the tank. But before his finger touched the switch, he jerked his hand away. What if he got another shock?

The light clicked on and off again. Scott stood by the tank. Waiting. But this time it didn't flash on again.

Scott stood in total darkness. He wanted a light on in his room—now.

He stumbled over to the wall. As he felt his way toward the ceiling light's switch, a short burst of light flooded the room—as bright and as quick as a streak of lightening. And then a loud bang exploded in the room—as loud as a clap of thunder.

Scott whirled around to face the tank. He could hear the water churning.

Another flash of lightning shot through the water.

Then the lid began to rumble. And before Scott could move, the lid blasted from the tank and shot up to the ceiling with a *crash!*

About R. L. Stine

R. L. Stine, the creator of *Ghosts of Fear Street,* has written almost 100 scary novels for kids. The *Ghosts of Fear Street* series, like the *Fear Street* series, takes place in Shadyside and centers on the scary events that happen to people on Fear Street.

When he isn't writing, R. L. Stine likes to play pinball on his very own pinball machine, and explore New York City with his wife, Jane, and fifteen-year-old son, Matt.